# Dear Parent:
## Your child's love of reading starts here!

Every child learns to read in a different way and at his or her own speed. Some go back and forth between reading levels and read favorite books again and again. Others read through each level in order. You can help your young reader improve and become more confident by encouraging his or her own interests and abilities. From books your child reads with you to the first books he or she reads alone, there are I Can Read Books for every stage of reading:

### SHARED READING
Basic language, word repetition, and whimsical illustrations, ideal for sharing with your emergent reader

### BEGINNING READING
Short sentences, familiar words, and simple concepts for children eager to read on their own

### READING WITH HELP
Engaging stories, longer sentences, and language play for developing readers

### READING ALONE
Complex plots, challenging vocabulary, and high-interest topics for the independent reader

### ADVANCED READING
Short paragraphs, chapters, and exciting themes for the perfect bridge to chapter books

I Can Read Books have introduced children to the joy of reading since 1957. Featuring award-winning authors and illustrators and a fabulous cast of beloved characters, I Can Read Books set the standard for beginning readers.

A lifetime of discovery begins with the magical words "I Can Read!"

*Visit www.icanread.com for information
on enriching your child's reading experience.*

I Can Read Book® is a trademark of HarperCollins Publishers.

Library of Congress catalog card number: 2010929909

IBSN 978-0-06-168972-7 (trade bdg.)—ISBN 978-0-06-057419-2 (pbk.)

11 12 13 14 15 SCP 10 9 8 7 6 5 4 3 2 1    ❖    First Edition

# The Berenstain Bears®
## and the
# Shaggy Little Pony

## Jan & Mike Berenstain

**HARPER**

*An Imprint of HarperCollinsPublishers*

Sister and Brother were visiting their neighbor Farmer Ben. They liked to help him take care of the animals on his farm.

"Hello, cubs!" said Farmer Ben.
"I want you to meet someone new
on the farm."
He led them to a pen.
Inside was a shaggy little pony.

"Meet old Oscar," said Ben.

"He has just come to live here."

"He is so cute!" said Sister.

The cubs rubbed his nose.

Oscar blew gently on their hands.

"That means he likes you," Ben told them.

"Can we help take care of him?"

asked Brother.

"Of course," said Ben.

"I will show you how."

Brother and Sister gave water to Oscar.

They gave hay and feed to Oscar.

They washed Oscar.

They brushed Oscar.

They led him into the barn.

They cleaned out his stall.

They picked out his hooves.

"That was a lot of work," said Ben.

"You did a good job.

Would you like to ride Oscar now?"

"Ride him?" said Sister.

"Could we?" said Brother.

"Why not?" said Ben.

Ben put an old saddle and bridle on Oscar.

He had riding helmets for the cubs to wear.

First, Ben helped Sister up onto Oscar.

He led Oscar and Sister around the pen.

Oscar was very calm and quiet.

Then it was Brother's turn.

"That was fun!" said Brother.

"Can we do it again tomorrow?"
asked Sister.

"Why not?" said Farmer Ben.

Brother and Sister began to go
to the farm every day.
They took care of Oscar
and they rode Oscar.
Soon they could ride him
without any help.
They rode him all over the farm.

They loved Oscar

and they loved to ride him.

One day, the cubs saw a sign

on the side of Farmer Ben's barn:

"What does that mean?"
they asked Farmer Ben.
"There's going to be a riding show
for cubs, here," said Ben.
"The best riders will get prize ribbons."
"Can we be in the show?" they asked.
"Why not?" said Ben.

The next day, there were lots of riders and ponies at the farm.

Some of the ponies were very fancy.

Some of the riders wore fancy clothes.

Brother and Sister were worried.
How would they do
on their shaggy little pony?
"Don't worry," said Ben.
"Oscar will do fine."

The fancy ponies and the fancy riders
went first.

They rode around in front of the judges.

The judges watched how they rode.

But it was a windy day.

Leaves swirled around the ponies' legs.

The fancy ponies were scared.

They bucked and kicked.

The judges frowned

and made notes on their pads.

Then it was time

for Brother and Sister to ride.

They took turns on Oscar.

The wind and the leaves

did not bother Oscar.

He was quiet and calm.

He trotted in front of the judges.

The judges smiled and nodded.

All the ponies and riders lined up.

The judges brought out the prize ribbons.

Blue was for first place.

Red was for second place.

Yellow was for third place.

White was for fourth place.

Brother and Sister had their fingers crossed.

"I hope we get a ribbon," Sister said.

The judges pinned the blue ribbon
on Oscar's bridle.
Sister and Brother were tied
for first place!
"I told you nothing bothers old Oscar,"
said Farmer Ben.

Brother and Sister rubbed Oscar's nose.

Oscar blew gently on their hands.